STO

Books by David Cornel DeJong

THE HAPPY BIRTHDAY UMBRELLA

THE HAPPY BIRTHDAY EGG

The
Happy Birthday
Egg

The Happy Birthday Egg

by

David Cornel DeJong

Illustrated by

Harvey Weiss

An Atlantic Monthly Press Book

Little, Brown and Company · Boston · Toronto

Fondly, for Mary Ellen Moffitt,
my mother-in-law

LIBRARY OF CONGRESS CATALOG CARD NO. 62-12376

FIRST EDITION

ATLANTIC-LITTLE, BROWN BOOKS
ARE PUBLISHED BY
LITTLE, BROWN AND COMPANY
IN ASSOCIATION WITH
THE ATLANTIC MONTHLY PRESS

Published simultaneously in Canada
by Little, Brown & Company (Canada) Limited

PRINTED IN THE UNITED STATES OF AMERICA

The
Happy Birthday
Egg

CHAPTER ONE

YOUNG DAVID woke up with a start and rubbed his eyes. Alexander the Great was growling. It was so early in the morning that there wasn't much light, but David could see that the cat's tail was three times as thick as it should be. And he could see a face at his bedroom window.

It was a face with large black eyes and a funny beak, and there was a long, bare neck beneath it.

David jumped out of bed, and he and Alexander crept toward the window. Before they could reach the window the face disappeared. Nothing was there.

David said, "I think we'd better hurry outdoors."

Alexander went trotting ahead of him, out of the bedroom and down the stairs. The house was very quiet; everybody was still asleep.

When David caught up with Alexander, the cat was sniffing at two footprints in the garden beneath the bedroom window. At least, David thought they were footprints. They were large

4

and deep and shaped like thick V's. David had
never seen anything like them. He looked up at
his bedroom window. It must have been a very
tall creature if it could stand here and look in his
window.

5

When he looked down again, Alexander had stopped sniffing at the footprints. With his nose close to the ground Alexander moved across the grass. Alexander was very long, and very low, and he acted very important.

For a while David followed Alexander, but when the cat crossed into the tall grass behind the

house, he had to stop. The grass was wet with dew, and he was wearing only his pajamas.

David looked around him. He couldn't see any strange, tall creature anywhere. He could see only the white tip of Alexander's tail disappearing behind the garage.

The sun was climbing over the faraway trees, but the house stayed quiet. Father and Mother and the baby were all asleep. And at that moment David remembered his grandmother.

Grandmother had arrived on the midnight train, and even though today was her birthday, she was going to sleep late. After that, he and Grandmother were going to take a birthday walk beneath his wonderful yellow umbrella with the windows in it and the bells on it. And for a minute David was sad. He had no birthday present for her.

It was early, very early. It was too early to wake up Grandmother. He had to talk to someone about the face at his bedroom window. But who?

Then he remembered Mrs. Twill, the baby sit-

8

ter. Mrs. Twill lived on the other side of the town, and Mrs. Twill said that she always got up early with the robins.

Once more David looked all around him. Sure enough, the robins were already up. So Mrs. Twill should be up too. He would go at once and tell Mrs. Twill all about the face he and Alexander had seen at the window.

10

CHAPTER TWO

IN HIS BEDROOM David put on his clothes very quietly and properly. He tied his shoelaces very neatly, because Mrs. Twill was very fussy. Then he looked out of his window again, but he saw nothing, not even Alexander.

Once more he crept down the stairs. There, beside the front door, stood his wonderful birthday umbrella. It was all yellow, with purple fringes and bells and a flamingo handle and a red blinker tip. It was closed, so he couldn't see its four windows.

Every time David took a long walk, or called on his friends Mrs. Twill, Mr. Bim, Sam and Jack and Joe, he carried his wonderful umbrella, because they had all helped in making it.

But this time he didn't dare to take it. The ten silver bells Grandmother had sewn on the umbrella would tinkle and jangle and wake everyone. This morning he would have to go without it.

12

He walked down the path that crossed the field
in back of the house, and no matter how hard he
looked, he didn't see any tall creature, nor even

Alexander the Great. At the end of the path he came to Jack and Joe's Service Station and Greasing Palace. It was still closed. It was that early!

David walked down the very quiet, very empty main street, and when he came to Mr. Bim's Tailor Shop, he saw that it too was still closed. And so was Sam's Secondhand Shop. But when he came to Mrs. Twill's house, there was Mrs. Twill, up with the robins and trimming her rosebushes.

"Good morning, Mrs. Twill," David shouted.

"For goodness' sake, David," Mrs. Twill cried. "How come you're up so early, and where is your beautiful umbrella?"

14

It would take too long to tell about the umbrella, so he said, "Mrs. Twill, I'm up early because of a face at my window."

"A face at your window?" Mrs. Twill screamed. "Well, we had better sit down on the porch and you tell me all about it."

They sat down each on a rocker, and David told Mrs. Twill what he and Alexander had seen. While she listened, Mrs. Twill rocked faster and faster. But when he was all through, she stopped and said, "Oh David, I can't believe it."

So David told her the whole story once more.

"Oh, I believe you all right, David. Except it is so impossible," Mrs. Twill said this time. "Now tell me, did this creature have horns?"

16

"No," David answered.

"Ears or teeth, David?"

"I don't think so, Mrs. Twill."

"Well, hair then?"

David thought and shook his head. "No, just some funny fuzz and big eyes and a big nose, maybe."

"Ah-ha!" Mrs. Twill shouted and jumped up. "I know exactly what you saw." She ran into the house and came back with a large stuffed bird on a wooden stand. The bird had a red silk ribbon with a large bow tied around it. It was a goose.

"It was this you saw, David. A goose," Mrs. Twill said.

"Oh no, Mrs. Twill," David cried.

"Well, maybe you can't see it right. It's the ribbon." And Mrs. Twill took off the red ribbon, and hung it around her own neck. "Now, isn't this what you saw, David?"

"Oh no, it was very tall and it had no feathers on its neck, Mrs. Twill."

"Dear me," Mrs. Twill sighed. "I was so hoping it was only a goose. But you say it was standing on the ground and it looked right in your upstairs window? Now let me think."

At last she said, "I think I'm coming right with you to your house and we'll see what we can see. It might be dangerous," Mrs. Twill said. "So I'd better bring these garden shears, and maybe a broom. That would help, don't you think, David?"

"Well, maybe, Mrs. Twill," David answered, but he wasn't at all sure.

CHAPTER THREE

DAVID and Mrs. Twill walked down the main street. Mrs. Twill carried her garden shears and a broom. She still had around her neck the red ribbon she had taken off the stuffed goose, and she talked every step of the way.

Sam was in front of his secondhand shop,

sweeping his sidewalk. Sam's shop was always cluttered and dusty, but David knew that Sam swept his sidewalk at least ten times a day.

When Sam saw them, he shouted, "Why, if it isn't my little friend Davie. But Davie without his great umbrella."

Mrs. Twill cried, "This is no time for small talk, Sam. This is a very serious business. A terrible creature was at David's window. It was all eyes and no hair."

"All eyes and no hair?" Sam shouted. "Oh my."

"You tell Sam all about it," Mrs. Twill said.

So David told Sam what he and Alexander had seen.

22

Sam listened with his head first on one side, then on the other. When David was finished, he said, "So, so, Davie. No hair, no feathers, no ears, no horns, no teeth. And very tall. What could it be? But wait! I have an idea. I know exactly what it was."

Sam hurried into his shop, and David and Mrs.

Twill followed him inside. The shop looked so dusty that Mrs. Twill started sweeping it up at once with her broom.

Sam shouted, "Ah but Mrs. Twill, that's just a little clean dirt. Why bother? Why not just take a look at this."

Sam had lifted something from a dark corner in the shop. It had a long neck and was all spotted. It was something that had come off a merry-go-round. "It's a giraffe," Sam said. "That's what you and Alexander saw, Davie."

"Oh no, Sam," David answered. "It had no fur, no ears, no knobs on top of its head."

"Are you very sure, Davie?" Sam asked, disappointed.

24

David hated to see Sam look so disappointed.
So he lay down on an old dusty sleigh, and he
looked at the giraffe Sam was holding up. It was
almost like lying in bed and looking at the window. Even so, the giraffe didn't look right at all.
Those ears and knobs were all wrong.

26

"No, Sam, it wasn't a giraffe," David said, getting up and letting Mrs. Twill brush him off.

"In that case," Sam said, "I'd better come along with you and Mrs. Twill. I'll lock up my shop."

Sam went to the wall and took down a very old gun with a long barrel. "It's a real weapon, better than a broom or a pair of shears any time," Sam said. "Except it has no ammunition."

Both Mrs. Twill and Sam looked very grim now. But David didn't. After all, the face at the window hadn't looked very dangerous.

CHAPTER FOUR

THEY DID NOT get very far. When David and Sam and Mrs. Twill came past Mr. Bim's Tailor Shop, there was Mr. Bim leaning out of his bedroom window above the shop. Mr. Bim looked sleepy and worried, and his little black beard was ruffled.

"What is this, David?" Mr. Bim called.

"Good morning, Mr. Bim," David said politely.

"Oh I know," Mr. Bim cried. "You are celebrating Mrs. Twill's birthday. She has a red ribbon around her neck."

"It's nothing of the kind," Mrs. Twill answered. "It is something much more serious. David, you'd better tell Mr. Bim at once about that terrible beast that tried to climb in your window. At once."

"It didn't try to climb in. It just looked in," David said. So then he told Mr. Bim all about it. Mr. Bim looked puzzled, and he leaned farther and farther out the window. His black beard seemed to point and wiggle more and more.

"But that makes no sense, David," Mr. Bim said at last. "Now just what did that thing really look like?"

It was funny, but Mr. Bim, with his big glasses and his funny little beard, looked much more like the face at his window than anything David had seen. But he couldn't say that to Mr. Bim. "Well," he said, "big eyes, and fuzz, and maybe a nose."

But David could see that Mr. Bim wasn't listening any longer. Mr. Bim had an idea, too. And sure enough Mr. Bim cried, "Oh, I know exactly what you saw, David. Just wait till I get some clothes on and I'll come downstairs and show you. Right in my tailor shop, I'll show you."

In a minute Mr. Bim opened the door of his tailor shop. He was holding a picture of a very tall man with very long legs. "Do you see what it is, David?" Mr. Bim asked. "It is a man on stilts you saw looking in your window, David."

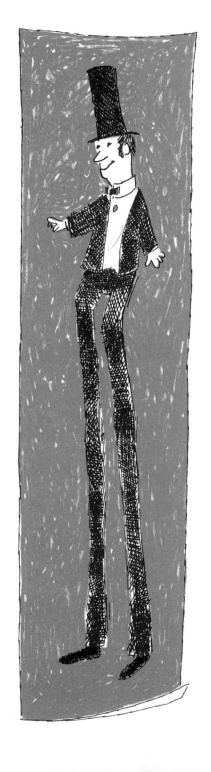

David shook his head. "No, it was not a man."

"I tell you it was a creature out of this world," Sam said.

"Dear me," Mr. Bim cried. "And I was so sure. And now I am sure I'd better come with you, but I need a weapon, too." He picked up a yardstick, and then another yardstick. "I think two are better than one, don't you, David?" he asked.

David didn't know what to say. Two yard-sticks didn't look like much. But he was quite sure that the face at his window had looked friendly.

CHAPTER FIVE

THEY ALL marched down the sidewalk. As they came to the end of the block, Jack and Joe drove up in their blue truck to open up their service station. "Well, Davie, what is all this about?" Jack shouted.

35

"Did somebody steal your beautiful umbrella?" Joe asked.

"David, you'd better tell Jack and Joe all about
the terrible thing that happened to you," said
Mrs. Twill.

So once more David told what he and Alexander had seen.

Jack and Joe listened very seriously.

"Oh, but we know what you saw, Davie, don't
we, Joe?" Jack said.

"We sure do," Joe said. "Step right into our
service station, ladies and gentlemen, and take
a look at our calendar."

Hanging inside the service station there was
a very large calendar and on it was a picture of

JULY

1	2	3	4	5	6	7
8	9	10	11	12	13	14
15	16	17	18	19	20	21
22	23	24	25	26	27	28
29	30	31				

three pairs of long, skinny legs, holding up piles of feathers and plumes, all gray and white and black. Growing out of all those feathers were long, naked necks that went down into the sand. There were no heads; they were buried in the sand.

"What you saw was an ostrich, Davie," Jack and Joe said.

David looked very hard at the picture. At his window he had seen a small head on a very long neck. Here he could see no heads at all.

"I don't know," he said. "The heads are in the sand."

"Humph," Mrs. Twill said, "who ever saw an ostrich in our town? No, I'm sure it was a monster David saw. We'd better be very careful."

"Still, I heard somewhere there's a man who's trying to raise ostriches in the next county," Joe said.

"You heard nothing of the kind, I'm sure," Mrs. Twill said. "Because I would have heard it, too. I pretty near always hear things first. I tell you, it's a dragon." And Mrs. Twill looked very fierce with her broom and her garden shears.

Now Jack grabbed a shovel and Joe a rake. "Let's go," they both said. "Let's take care of that monster."

They marched single file down the path that led through the field to David's house. Joe walked ahead because he was the strongest, then came

Mr. Bim, and then Mrs. Twill. Next came David because he was the smallest and had no weapon. Behind him came Sam, and then Jack, who was the second strongest.

When they passed a large white rock, Alexander looked out at them, round-eyed with surprise. As they marched on toward the house,

Alexander went scampering ahead of them all, with his tail raised.

"We'd better be very quiet. Grandmother is asleep and it is her birthday," David warned them.

"We've got to be very quiet so we can sneak up on that monster," Mr. Bim said.

Very quietly they crept around the corner of the house, and David showed them the footprints. "I told you," Mrs. Twill whispered. "I knew it all the time. Those footprints were made by a dragon."

Then they all watched as Mr. Bim took his two yardsticks and carefully measured from the garden up to David's window. "It is seven feet and two inches," he said. "Now what is seven feet and two inches tall and has no hair and big eyes?"

"A dragon, of course," Mrs. Twill whispered.

CHAPTER SIX

DAVID said nothing. He was watching Alexander the Great. Alexander sniffed at the footprints once more and stalked toward the back of the house. He acted as if he knew exactly what he was doing. "I think Alexander knows where it is," David whispered.

On tiptoe they all followed Alexander, David first and Mrs. Twill last, all the time looking over her shoulder for a dragon.

Alexander led them first to the garage, then in back of the garage and under the grape arbor. There he stopped, sniffed the air, and swished his tail. And suddenly they all saw it.

It was something large and white and round. David reached Alexander first. His cat was sniffing at a very, very large egg. Near the egg lay a beautiful feather. A plume. Mr. Bim and Sam and Jack and Joe and, last of all, Mrs. Twill looked at the large egg and the beautiful feather.

"I knew it. I knew it all the time. It's a dragon's egg," Mrs. Twill cried and raised her broom.

44

"Any moment now the dragon will get us. Especially if we touch that egg."

"Dragons don't have feathers, Mrs. Twill," Mr. Bim said.

"How do you know?" Mrs. Twill shouted, and

this time she shook her garden shears. "We're in real danger."

She made them all so excited that Jack and Joe started pointing their shovel and rake like swords, and Sam pointed his old gun, even though there was nothing to aim at except some clusters of green grapes. But Mr. Bim took his two yardsticks, and with one he measured the egg, and with the other the feather.

Mr. Bim said to David, "It's an ostrich egg all right. And it's an ostrich feather, too, I just know."

"Well, where then is the ostrich?" Mrs. Twill cried, waving both her shears and her broom.

"Ah, but I know," Sam said, at last lowering his old gun. "Long ago I read a book in my shop. And that book said that ostriches always lay their eggs in secret places, and then they run off, back where they came from. Except that right now I'm not sure if the book was about ostriches, or penguins, or pelicans."

This time Mrs. Twill shouted: "Of course, that

isn't a pelican or penguin's egg. How silly of you, Sam. And I'm sure now it was an ostrich, because once upon a time I had a hat that had an ostrich plume on it just like that." Mrs. Twill dropped her two weapons and giggled, as if all the time she hadn't been afraid at all.

But nobody noticed that Grandmother had come out of the house and was standing on the back porch wondering what all the excitement was about so early in the day.

Only David saw her. And then David knew. Here was a wonderful surprise for Grandmother. A wonderful birthday present, and it wouldn't even matter to Grandmother whether it was a pelican, a penguin, or an ostrich egg. Or for that

matter a dragon egg. He got so excited, he shouted, "It's for Grandmother. A surprise for Grandmother's birthday!"

"My goodness, David," Mrs. Twill chattered. "I knew it all the time. I put this red ribbon around my neck for a good reason all the time."

Jack and Joe lifted the large egg from the ground. Sam and Mr. Bim lifted the ostrich feather together as if it were just as heavy as the egg. Mrs. Twill took the red ribbon from her neck, and then all five carefully tied the ribbon around the egg, and tucked the plume in the bow of the ribbon.

In the meantime, Father and Mother had come out of the house, too, and were standing beside

Grandmother watching all the strange doings beneath the grape arbor.

Joe now put the large egg with its red ribbon and white plume carefully in David's hands. Once more, with David in front, Mrs. Twill next, then Sam and Mr. Bim, and Jack and Joe last because they sang the loudest, they marched. They were all singing, "Happy birthday, dear Grandmother. Happy birthday to you," as they marched up to Grandmother on the back porch.

Then Father and Mother started singing, too, and their eyes were round with surprise looking at the strange and wonderful gift David was carrying for Grandmother.

2113